AESOP'S FABLES

Town Mouse and Country Mouse

Adapted by Ronne Randall
Illustrated by Louise Gardner

Bright ☆ Sparks

Once there was a roly-poly, wiggly-whiskered mouse, who lived in a snug little nest under an oak tree.

Country Mouse loved his home. He had plenty of acorns, nuts and berries to eat and a warm and cosy straw bed to sleep in.

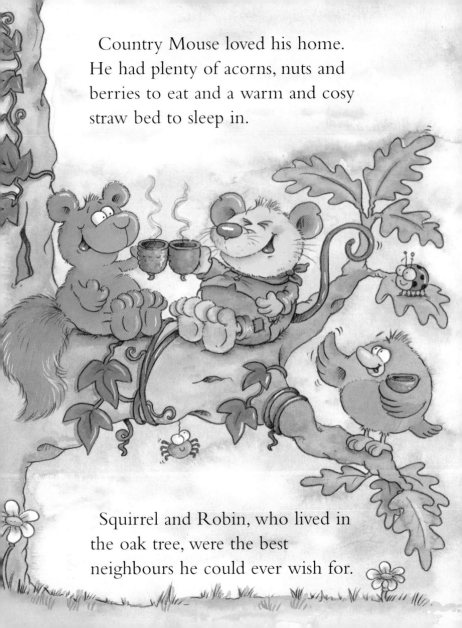

Squirrel and Robin, who lived in the oak tree, were the best neighbours he could ever wish for.

One day, Country Mouse had a
surprise. His cousin, Town Mouse,
came to visit from the Big City.

Town Mouse was sleek and slender,
with a smooth, shiny coat. His whiskers
were smart and elegant.

Country Mouse felt a little ordinary beside him. But he didn't mind. All he wanted to do was to make Town Mouse feel welcome.

"Are you hungry, cousin?" he said. "Come and have some supper!"

But Town Mouse didn't like the
acorns and blackberries that
Country Mouse gave him to eat.
They were tough and sour.

Home
Sweet
Home

And Town Mouse thought
his cousin's friends were boring.

The straw bed that he slept in that night was so rough and scratchy, that he didn't sleep a wink!

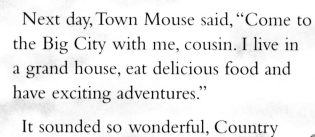

Next day, Town Mouse said, "Come to the Big City with me, cousin. I live in a grand house, eat delicious food and have exciting adventures."

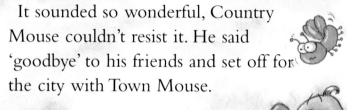

It sounded so wonderful, Country Mouse couldn't resist it. He said 'goodbye' to his friends and set off for the city with Town Mouse.

After a long journey, the two mice could see the Big City and, even though he was very tired, Country Mouse was really excited.

When they arrived in the Big City, Country Mouse was frightened. It was *so* noisy – horns blared and wheels clattered all around them. Huge lorries roared and rumbled down the street and the smelly, smoky air made them choke and cough.

And there were dogs *everywhere*!

At last, they arrived safely at Town Mouse's house.

It was very grand, just as Town Mouse had said. But it was *so* big!

Country Mouse was afraid
that he would get lost!

"Don't worry," said Town Mouse to Country Mouse. "You'll soon find your way around the house. For now, just stay close to me. I'm starving—let's go and have a snack."

Country Mouse was hungry, too, so
he followed his cousin to the kitchen.

Country Mouse had never seen so much delicious food – there were plates full of fruit, nuts, cheese and cakes.

He and his cousin ate and ate and ate!

But Country Mouse wasn't used to
this sort of rich food. Before he knew
it, his tummy was aching.

Suddenly, a huge woman came into the room.
"Eek! Mice!" she screamed.

She grabbed a big broom and began to swat the mice, who scampered off as fast as they could.

As the two mice scurried across the floor, Country Mouse thought things couldn't possibly get worse. But how wrong he was!

A big cat suddenly sprang out from behind a chair! With a loud **"M-E-E-O-O-W-W,"** he pounced on the two little mice.

Country Mouse had never been so frightened. He darted and dashed as fast as his aching tummy would let him.

The two mice jumped through a mousehole and were safe at last in Town Mouse's house.

"Phew! I think we've done enough for one day," said Town Mouse, when they had caught their breath.

"Let's get some sleep," he said, with a yawn. "I'll show you the rest of the house in the morning."

Country Mouse curled up in the hard little bed. But he was too frightened and unhappy to sleep. As he listened to his cousin snore, he tried hard not to cry.

Next morning, Town Mouse was ready for more adventures, but Country Mouse had had more than enough.

"Thank you for inviting me," he told his cousin, "but I have seen all I want to see of the Big City. It is too big and noisy and dirty—and too full of danger for me. I want to go back to my quiet, peaceful home in the country."

So, Country Mouse went back to his snug, cosy home under the oak tree. He had never been so happy to see his friends—and they wanted to hear all about his adventures.

Country Mouse was pleased to tell them everything that had happened in the Big City—but he *never, ever* went back there again!